English text © 2001 Chronicle Books.
English text design by Jessica Dacher.
Typeset in Blue Century.
Printed in China.

Library of Congress Cataloging-in-Publication Data
Ardalan, Haydé.
[Milton chez le vétérinaire. English]
Milton goes to the vet / by Haydé Ardalan.
p. cm.
Summary: A reluctant cat is taken to the veterinarian for an examination.
ISBN 0-8118-2843-3
1. Cats—Juvenile fiction. [1. Cats—Fiction. 2.
Veterinarians—Fiction.] I. Title.
PZ10.3.A75 Mi 2001
[E]--dc21
00-012267

Distributed in Canada by Raincoast Books
9050 Shaughnessy Street, Vancouver, British Columbia V6P 6E5

10 9 8 7 6 5 4 3 2 1

Chronicle Books LLC
85 Second Street
San Francisco, California 94105

www.chroniclebooks.com

Milton
Goes to the Vet

by Haydé Ardalan

chronicle books · san francisco

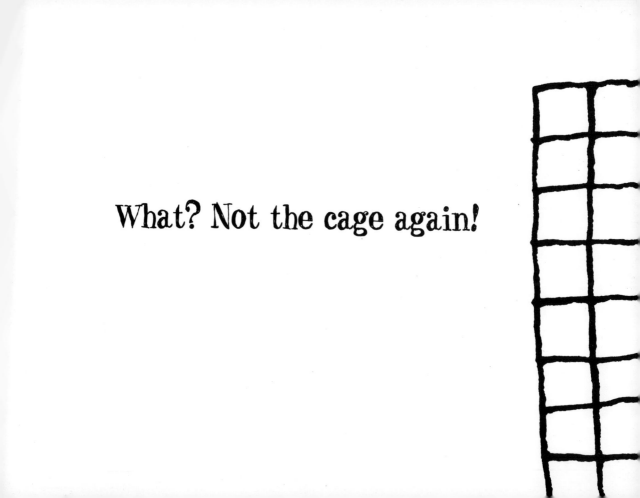

What? Not the cage again!

Quick, hide!

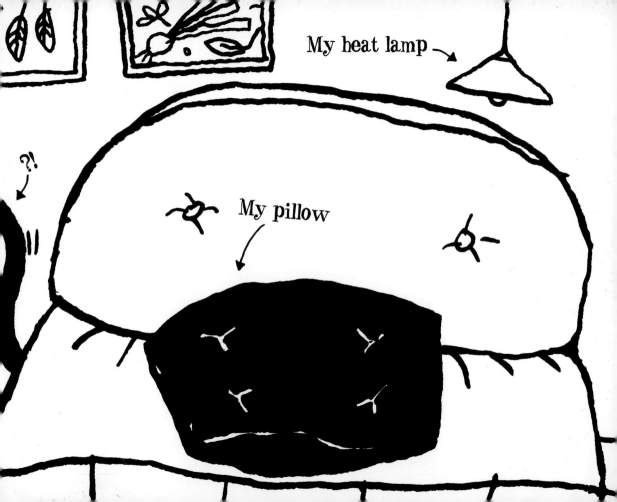

They always find me in the end.

I've seen this neighborhood before.

Destination: the vet.

I don't belong here with these animals.

What torture awaits me?

Hold on for dear life!

Now I'm in for it.

Aieee! I've been hit!

Nice clean, sharp teeth.

Good for biting.

I'll let myself out, thank you.

No more treats?

After all that, it was nothing!

This looks familiar.

Destination: home.

That bird will keep a minute.
Right now I could use a nap.

Praise for *Milton:*

"Milton is highly pleased with himself and very amusing." — *New York Times*

"Feline fanciers will delight in this sophisticated account of a self-confident cat." — *Parenting*

"[Milton] will please not only children but also adults who love cats." — *Chicago Tribune*

Praise for *Milton's Christmas:*

"The tongue-in-cheek text wittily counters the mayhem in the drawings." — *Publishers Weekly*

"Whether he's chasing decorations or snooping under the tree, his antics are sure to charm anyone who's enjoyed the holidays with a cat." — *Cat Fancy*

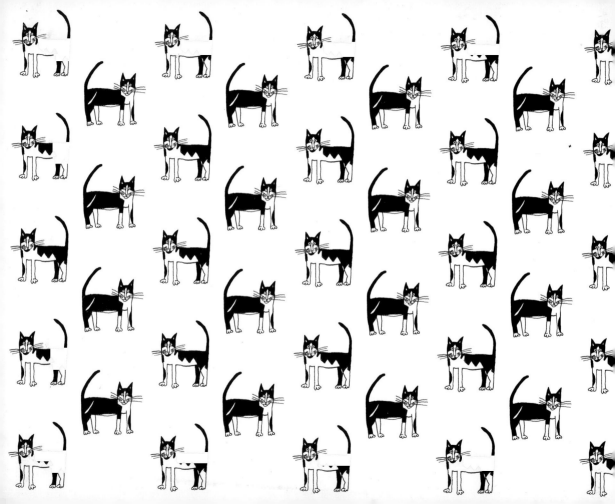